Potatoes, Potatoes

By Anita Lobel

Greenwillow Books

An Imprint of HarperCollinsPublishers

First published in 1967 by Harper & Row, Publishers, Inc.

Reissued in 2004 by Greenwillow Books, an imprint of HarperCollins Publishers.

Watercolors were used to prepare the full-color art.

The text type is 16-point Revival 555.

The Library of Congress catalogued an earlier edition as follows:

Lobel, Anita.

Potatoes, Potatoes / by Anita Lobel.

Summary: Recounts how a mother's love and potatoes ended the war.

ISBN 0-06-023927-1 (trade). ISBN 0-06-023928-X (lib. bdg.)

PZ7.L7794 Po [Fic] 67-016231

Reissued edition, 2004:

ISBN 0-06-051817-0 (trade); ISBN 0-06-051818-9 (lib. bdg.)

10 9 8 7 6 5 4 3 2 1

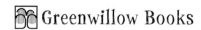

Greenwillow Books

For Virginia, Steve,
and Paul, my new
family under the
old willow tree

Long ago there were two countries,
one in the east, the other in the west.
One day they started a war with each other.
No one had time to take care of the fields
or the cows or the chickens.
And between battles the people spent all their time
polishing swords, making cannonballs,
and sewing buttons on soldiers' uniforms.

In a valley between these two countries
lived a woman who did not bother with the war.
She had two sons.
She had a cow, some chickens,
and a large potato field.
To protect her potatoes and her boys from the war,
she built a wall around everything she owned.

The boys loved their mother.
They helped to plant, weed,
and harvest the potatoes.
They took care of the animals.
They liked their soft beds
and their cozy house.
"But why must we have a wall
around us?" they sometimes asked.
"Because my potatoes will not grow
if the winds from the east and the
west blow on them,"
their mother would answer.

On cold winter nights when storms and battles raged outside,
they baked their potatoes in a fire and ate them.

But the two sons grew up.

One day the older son looked toward the east and saw a regiment of soldiers marching by.

"Mother, look at the red uniforms and beautiful swords," he cried, dropping his potato sack.

"I have seen red uniforms tattered and muddy, and swords bent and broken," his mother answered. "Please, don't bother me and go back to your work! We'll have boiled potatoes with sour cream for dinner."

"I am tired of planting potatoes," cried her son. "Good-bye, Mother."

And he ran off toward the east.

The next day the younger son looked toward the
west and saw a regiment of soldiers marching by.
"Mother, look at the blue uniforms and the shiny
medals," he cried, dropping his spade.
"I have seen blue uniforms torn and stained
with blood, and medals rusting in the fields.
Do your work now," pleaded his mother.
"I'll make you some potato pancakes later."
"I am tired of weeding potatoes," said her son.
"Good-bye, Mother."
And he ran off toward the west.
Left all alone, the woman cried bitterly.
Then she bolted her door
and went back to the potato field.

The two sons liked being soldiers.
Their uniforms were new.
Their swords and medals gleamed.
Ladies threw flowers as they
marched by.
One son became a general
in the army of the east,
and the other a commander
in the army of the west.

Many battles were fought.
But sometimes after a battle
the general looked
at his muddied uniform
and bent sword,
and thought of a baked potato
and a soft bed.

And sometimes the commander
looked at his stained uniform
and rusting medals,
and thought of potato-planting
and a warm fire.
They thought of their mother
and felt sad.

Still more battles were fought.
The fields were empty and burned.
There was nothing left to eat in the east or the west.

"We are hungry," cried all the soldiers
in the army of the east.
Their general knew a place
where there was food.

"We want food," demanded all the soldiers
in the army of the west.
Their commander knew a place
where there were things to eat.

One night the two armies marched toward the valley

where the woman and the potatoes were.

"Mother, my soldiers are hungry," cried the older son
over the eastern wall. "We must be strong to win battles!"
"Mother, my men want food," cried the younger son
over the western wall. "Let us have some potatoes,
and we shall fight for victory!"

There was stony silence behind the wall.
"Potatoes, potatoes!" the soldiers began to shout.
"POTATOES! POTATOES! POTATOES! POTATOES!
Let us break down the wall and get the potatoes!"

From the east and the west the two armies crashed through the wall.

A furious battle for the potatoes began.

Soon the wall had tumbled down.
The house lay in ruins.
The cow and the chickens were gone.
The field was trampled.
Many soldiers were moaning on the ground.
And the general and the commander had been wounded.
Behind a large pile of rubble
the woman lay on the ground, without moving.
The general and the commander looked at their mother
and all the broken things, and began to weep.

"Mother, Mother, this is our fault!" cried the older son.

"What have we done?" cried the younger son.

"Speak to us! Speak to us!" they begged.

The battle had stopped,
and the soldiers stood very still.
They looked at the crying general.
They looked at the crying commander.
They thought of their own mothers.
And all the soldiers began to cry.

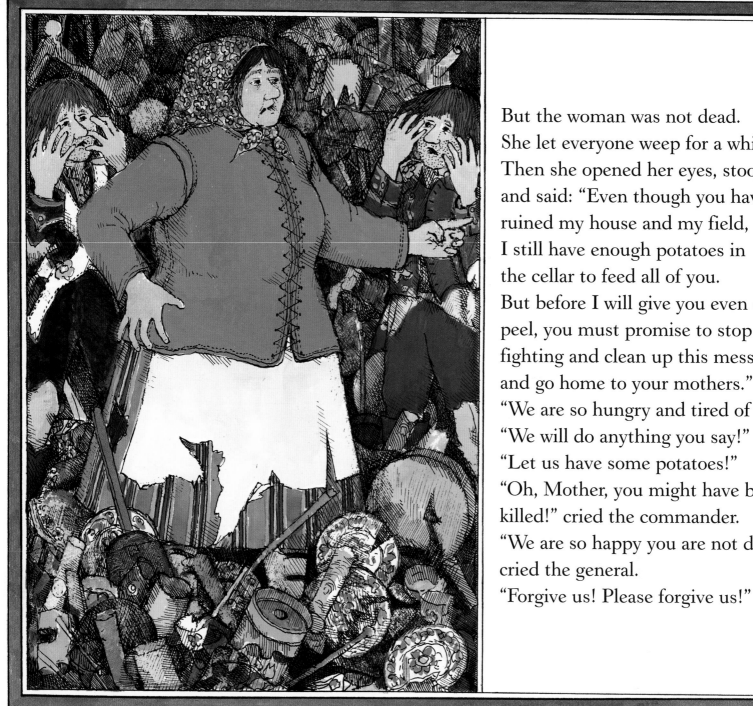

But the woman was not dead.
She let everyone weep for a while.
Then she opened her eyes, stood up,
and said: "Even though you have
ruined my house and my field,
I still have enough potatoes in
the cellar to feed all of you.
But before I will give you even one
peel, you must promise to stop all the
fighting and clean up this mess,
and go home to your mothers."
"We are so hungry and tired of fighting!"
"We will do anything you say!"
"Let us have some potatoes!"
"Oh, Mother, you might have been
killed!" cried the commander.
"We are so happy you are not dead!"
cried the general.
"Forgive us! Please forgive us!"

"Hurrah for potatoes and hurrah for mothers!" shouted the soldiers
when they had eaten and felt better.

They began to sing songs their mothers had taught them.
Soon the singing was heard in the east and in the west.

Many mothers found their sons. Everywhere mothers and sons fell into each other's arms.
Then they thanked the woman for the good potatoes and said good-bye.

They went home to the east and home to the west. The soldiers took off their uniforms and told the people to stop polishing swords and making cannonballs.

The two sons buried their swords and medals.
They helped their mother plant new potatoes in the field.
They rebuilt their mother's house and mended the broken things.

But they did not rebuild the wall.